MR. SILLY
gets the giggles

Original concept by Roger Hargreaves
Illustrated and written by Adam Hargreaves

MR. MEN **LITTLE MISS**

MR. MEN™ LITTLE MISS™ © THOIP (a SANRIO company)

Mr. Silly gets the giggles © 1998 THOIP (a Sanrio company)
Printed and published under licence from Price Stern Sloan, Inc., Los Angeles.
This edition published in 2017 by Dean, an imprint of Egmont UK Limited,
The Yellow Building, 1 Nicholas Road, London W11 4AN

ISBN 978 0 6035 7411 5
68475/1
Printed in Estonia

Mr Silly lives in a place called Nonsenseland where the grass is blue and the trees are red. Which you already know.

It is also a place where zebra crossings are spotty. Which you probably did not know.

In Nonsenseland you post letters in telephone boxes and you make phone calls from letter boxes.

And in Nonsenseland the umbrellas all have holes in them so that you know when it has stopped raining.

Which is utter nonsense, but not if your name is Mr Silly.

Now, one morning, last week, Mr Silly got up, put on his hat, brushed his teeth with soap, as usual, polished his shoes with toothpaste, as usual, and went down to breakfast.

For breakfast Mr Silly had fried eggs and custard, as usual, and a cup of hot, milky marmalade, as usual.

After breakfast he went out into his garden. The day before Mr Silly had bought a tree, but as he looked at the tree he realised that he did not have a hole to plant it in.

So he went to the hardware shop.

"Good morning," said Mr Silly. "I would like to buy a hole."

"Sorry," said the sales assistant, "we're all out of holes. Sold the last one yesterday."

"Bother," said Mr Silly.

He decided there was nothing for it but to go in search of a hole.

He walked and he walked and he walked.

Eventually Mr Silly stopped walking and looked down at his feet.

"That's odd," he said, "this grass is green."

"Of course it is," said a voice behind him.

"Grass is always green."

"Who are you?" asked Mr Silly.

"Little Miss Wise."

"I'm Mr Silly. Could you tell me where I am?"

"You're in Sensibleland," said Miss Wise.

Mr Silly had walked so far that he had walked right out of Nonsenseland.

"I'm looking for a hardware shop," said Mr Silly. "Can you help?"

"Certainly," said Miss Wise. "Follow me."

As they walked along Mr Silly looked about him.

He had never seen anywhere like it. The grass was green, the trees were green, even the hedges were green.

They came to a zebra crossing. A stripey zebra crossing.

Mr Silly chuckled, and then he giggled and then he laughed out loud.

"Why are you laughing?" asked Miss Wise.

"The ...hee hee...zebra crossing...ha ha...is stripey," laughed Mr Silly.

"What else would a zebra crossing be?" said Miss Wise.

"Spotty! Of course!" said Mr Silly, wiping the tears from his eyes.

"How silly," said Miss Wise.

They set off again and the further they went the more Mr Silly laughed.

He laughed when he saw someone posting a letter in a letterbox.

He laughed when he saw someone using a phone in a telephone box.

And he laughed when he saw an umbrella without holes in it.

Eventually they came to Miss Bolt's Hardware Shop

"Good afternoon," said Mr Silly. "I would like to buy a hole."

"A hole?" questioned Miss Bolt.

"Yes, big enough to plant a tree in," explained Mr Silly.

Miss Bolt sniggered.

Miss Wise chortled.

And then they burst out laughing.

"I've never heard anything so absurd," laughed Miss Bolt.

"But I do have something that may help, though."

That evening Mr Silly invited his friend Mr Nonsense for supper and told him all about his day in Sensibleland.

Mr Nonsense laughed so hard he fell off his chair!

"...and then," continued Mr Silly, "Miss Bolt gave me a spade. A spade! Why in the world would I want to buy a spade when all I wanted was a hole!"

"Heehee...that's...ha ha...ridiculous!" laughed Mr Nonsense.

"What's for pudding?"

"Spam roly poly," answered Mr Silly.

"Oh goody," said Mr Nonsense.
"My favourite."